Murder during the Mistletoe Procession

A Little Firling Mystery – Book Five

by Belinda Chavremootoo

Dedication

For every cat who ever solved a mystery quietly before the humans caught up.

Text Copyright

About the Author

Belinda writes layered mysteries where memory lingers, landscapes remember, and silence speaks louder than words. Her stories slip between the literary and the intimate—part atmospheric suspense, part quiet reckoning. Rooted in a love for islands, history, and hidden truths, her work invites readers to linger in the in-between.

She believes some lands carry echoes of everything they've witnessed—grief, joy, betrayal—and that nostalgia for a place is its own kind of story.

She also writes heartfelt children's stories that whisper courage into quiet hearts. With magical ladybugs, story-saving oaks, and brave little girls like Maia, Belinda hopes to help young readers find their own voice—and use it boldly.

When she's not writing, Belinda tends to her garden, guided by the rustle of leaves, the smell of earth, and the quiet company of two cats who always seem to know more than they let on.

Coming Soon…

Murder in Three Movements

A Little Firling Mystery — Book Six

Little Firling is ready to welcome spring with blooming garlands, tangled ribbons, and a friendly rivalry that's anything but friendly.

But when festival darling Julian Parrish falls to his death beneath a tent of silks and secrets, the celebration comes undone.

Whispers begin to swirl:

Was it the pressure of competition? A romantic grudge?

Or something far more dangerous, buried deep in the orchard and tied with a ribbon no one dares untangle?

Annabel, Evie, and Persephone are back—armed with questions, tea, and an increasing number of suspects.

Because in a village where the past is always in bloom...

One vanished.

One warned.

One watched.

And now, the truth is ready to bloom.

Featuring:

- A maypole with more tension than ribbon

- A secret too heavy for spring air

- And a cat with claws aimed at justice

Table of Contents

Prologue

She folded the ribboned reply into the inner pocket of her coat.

Then, she looked around the chapel one last time, unaware that someone else had already been inside.

That a candle had burned longer than the rest.

That a cold draft curled under the door.

That a shadow had not waited for her to leave...

But had come for her.

Quietly.

Carefully.

When the chapel doors opened again, it wasn't Agnes who moved them.

Outside, the snow fell gently.

The mistletoe crown was still in her hand.

And in the frost behind her—

Footprints.

But only one set.

Before the fall of snow, there was a moment of stillness. And every secret was still in place.

Chapter 1

The first snow fell like it had been waiting politely all morning.

It didn't blanket the village in drama—just a soft veil across rooftops, hedges, and the tips of boots outside the chapel. The kind of snow that whispered: *soon.*

Agnes Thorne stood beneath the arch of the chapel doorway, one gloved hand resting on the cold stone. She wasn't waiting for anyone in particular. She just liked to see the snow arrive.

At seventy-three, Agnes moved slower than she once had, but there was something about her stillness that made people listen. She'd lived in Little Firling long enough to become part of its fabric—the sort of person whose name appeared in stories told by three generations, often in the same breath.

She wore a charcoal-grey coat with a plum shawl tucked neatly under the collar, her brooch—the same frosted holly pin she wore every December—glinting at her shoulder. Her white hair was twisted into a bun that had survived a thousand winter gales and a thousand more rehearsals.

Today was her last.

Not that she'd said so. People would know. Agnes had been the Spirit of the Season for thirty-seven years. She'd led more processions than anyone could count, handwoven more mistletoe crowns than the village trees could grow. This year, she would pass the role on. Quietly. Gracefully.

But not today.

Today was the rehearsal.

And the rehearsal mattered.

"Morning, Agnes," called Nora from the bookshop, arms full of hymn sheets and barely-balanced mince pies. "You're here early."

"I like to open the chapel doors," Agnes replied with a soft smile. "It lets the warmth remember how to find its way in."

Children's laughter rang out across the green as the Snowdrop Circle dashed toward the chapel, scarves askew and glitter clinging to everything. Rosie ran ahead, trailing a paper star; Theo followed, muttering to himself about forgotten lines. Millie, James, and Pippa joined soon after, their breath fogging in the air like smoke from invisible lanterns.

Agnes greeted each child by name. Her voice was gentle, but her presence stilled even the rowdiest scarf.

She turned just as the chapel bell gave a single chime.

Not the hour.

Just... one.

And that's when she saw her.

Persephone.

The cat padded silently across the path, tail high, black coat dappled with snowflakes like she'd been kissed by winter. She paused at Agnes's feet and looked up—one long blink, then another.

Agnes knelt, slowly.

"You're early too."

Persephone blinked again. Then, without ceremony, she trotted inside.

Agnes stood with a wince she didn't show. Her fingers hovered near her coat pocket for a moment, then dropped. She followed the cat into the chapel.

***

Inside, the chapel glowed.

Not brightly, but steadily. Light from the stained-glass windows splashed colour across the stone floor, the saints watching as they always did—silent, fractured, waiting.

A cluster of children sat cross-legged near the front pews, clutching half-eaten biscuits and star-shaped crafts that looked like melting galaxies.

Every winter, just before the Procession, Agnes gathered her *Snowdrop Circle*—always a handful, never more than five—for what she called *seasonal settling*.

"We prepare the heart before we prepare the candles," she'd once said.

This year's circle wiggled and hushed and waited.

"Is this when we make the wish?" Rosie whispered.

Agnes smiled.

"Wishes can't be made on demand. They have to be ready."

And the children nodded like they understood.

Because with Agnes... they always did.

***

The doors opened again. A breeze followed.

"Sorry, sorry, we're not late—okay, we're a little late," Annabel called, balancing a tray of cranberry muffins like a waitress at a festive pub. Evie trailed behind her, eating a croissant and pretending it wasn't slightly frozen.

Persephone trotted toward them and then veered left, leaping onto the window ledge like a saint in fur.

Annabel smiled at Agnes, who nodded once, and went back to tying ribbon onto the mistletoe crown.

"Is it just me," Evie murmured, "or does she seem... I don't know. Quieter?"

"She's always quiet," Annabel said.

"No," Evie replied. "This is different. It's like she's already half a memory."

Before Annabel could answer, Barbara Ellington cleared her throat near the altar.

"If I could have everyone's attention—just briefly!"

The mood shifted. Even the candles braced.

"This year," Barbara said, "we're introducing a new element to the procession. A Wishing Box. Anyone can place a seasonal hope or memory inside, and it will be sealed and placed at the foot of the Virgin Mary and Child."

Groans. Rustling. A single sigh from the choir loft.

Barbara continued, chin high.

Agnes said nothing.

She was gazing at the statue in question.

The Virgin stood at the chapel's heart, hands cradling the child, eyes soft and unreadable. The stone beneath was worn smooth—from christenings, communions, weddings, funerals, and prayers whispered through the ache of living.

The chapel was old.

It remembered everything.

***

At the back, near the shadows, Grace Merrick watched it all unfold.

She hadn't meant to stay so long.

She hadn't meant to stay at all.

But then she saw Agnes. And her father's words returned like a forgotten song.

"She made the world feel gentler."

She didn't know if she believed in memory.

But watching Agnes now, her hand drifting over a mistletoe crown she'd likely tied in her sleep, she felt something settle and ache in her chest.

Not fear.

Not threat.

Just the quiet, terrible sense that *she
was already too late.*

***

The rehearsal ended with soft
applause and a few glitter-related
incidents.

People filtered out. Candles were
snuffed. Robes folded. Songs hummed
and then forgotten.

Annabel helped Nora gather sheet
music. Evie pinched two extra mince pies
and winked at a toddler in fairy wings.

Only one person remained.

Agnes stood in the pews, her shawl
over one arm, eyes on the statue.

The chapel was silent now.

She sat.

Her hand reached into her coat pocket.

Touched the ribboned letter.

She didn't take it out.

She didn't need to.

Tomorrow, she thought.

One miracle. Just one.

Outside, the bell rang once more.

The angelus.

Chapter 2

Rosie Harrington could only walk slowly for exactly five minutes at a time.

After that, her body instinctively broke into a gallop, a twirl, or a full sprint—usually at the most inconvenient moment.

"Rosie!" her mum called, a little breathless, a lot amused. "Stay where we can see you, love!"

But Rosie was already rounding the side of the chapel, the snow crunching softly under her boots.

It was the first proper snow of the season. Not just frost or flurries—*real snow*, the kind that settled and softened the world like a story was about to start.

The side path was narrow and winding, framed by low stone walls and half-buried winter flower beds. Rosie liked it best because no one else ever used it. It felt like her secret trail to somewhere important.

The chapel's side door sat in a little alcove, beneath the arched shadow of a stained-glass window. A bench curved along the wall nearby—people sat there in spring to feel the sun, or in summer to rest after weddings. In winter, it just waited.

That's when she saw the shawl.

It was lying on the second step. Plum-coloured. A little wet at the edges. Snow was settling on it like powdered sugar.

"Miss Agnes?"

She said it softly, not because she was scared, but because the moment felt wrapped in quiet.

She stepped closer.

And saw the shoes.

Just beneath the bench.

And then the mistletoe crown—tipped, its ribbon trailing toward the step below.

Rosie stopped moving.

Her breath caught in her chest.

Miss Agnes was sitting—or slumped, maybe—against the chapel wall, her hands resting in her lap, her head tilted slightly as if she'd been looking up at the sky when her eyes closed.

She didn't look cold.

She didn't look hurt. She looked like a statue.

Or a dream that had folded itself into the snow.

The shawl was beside her. *Not worn. Not wrapped.* Just... there.

Snow was still falling, light and steady, brushing against her coat, clinging to the folds of the mistletoe crown.

Rosie stared.

She's sleeping, she thought.

She's just very tired.

But Miss Agnes always opened her eyes when Rosie spoke.

Always.

Rosie's voice came out like paper. "Miss Agnes?"

Nothing.

Rosie blinked. She felt something rising in her throat that didn't feel like words.

The bell rang once—just once—from the square.

And Rosie screamed.

***

By the time Rosie's parents reached the steps, she was curled beside the wall, face white as frost, her mittened hands shaking.

"Rosie?" her mum whispered, dropping to her knees, pulling her close.

Her dad hovered behind them—silent, staring.

Because now they saw her too.

Agnes Thorne.

Still.

Her skin was cold, lips pale. Snow clinging to her sleeves, her hair, her lashes.

The mistletoe crown tilted gently near her feet.

Rosie's mother gasped, then looked away quickly—as if by not seeing, she could undo what had been seen.

"She's just—" her father started, then stopped.

There wasn't a word for it. Not yet.

And then someone else came running.

A villager from the square, coat unbuttoned, scarf half-on, eyes wide.

"What happened?"

Rosie's mother tried to explain, but her voice was full of ice.

"She's gone," someone whispered.

And that's when the others arrived.

More footsteps. More snow boots crunching.

More questions trailing behind them like breath in the cold.

"Wasn't she just at the rehearsal?"

“She looked fine…”

“It’s the cold, probably. Poor love.”

“She felt frozen. Like she’d already been there for hours.”

“She was old. It was her time.”

“At least it was peaceful.”

“She always loved that chapel.”

“Maybe she wanted to go there.”

“She wouldn’t have suffered. No pain. Just…”

“Just sleep.”

The words fluttered like snowflakes.

Soft. Well-meaning. *False.*

***

Annabel heard the commotion from halfway down the lane and started walking faster, then jogging.

Persephone was ahead of her.

Tail high. No hesitation.

And when Annabel turned the corner and saw the cluster of people around the side steps, her heart did something it hadn't done in years.

It dropped. Quietly. Like a candle going out.

She didn't push her way through.

She didn't need to.

Persephone was already there—sitting by the mistletoe crown. Not touching it. Not blinking. Just watching.

****

The murmurs were soft now.

No more questions.

Just sorrow, reshaped as comfort.

"She was old."

"It was peaceful."

"The way she would've wanted."

Annabel stood still; hands cold despite her gloves.

Persephone hadn't moved.

She sat at the edge of the steps, tail curled neatly, eyes fixed on the mistletoe crown.

Then came the voice. Low. Calm. Unmistakable.

"She wouldn't have left her shawl."

Annabel turned.

Benedict Harper stood behind her, coat buttoned to the neck, scarf tight, hands tucked into sensible woollen gloves. He wasn't hunched like most men his age. He moved like someone *who carried thoughts carefully.*

"She was always careful," he said, stepping forward.

"That shawl was a gift. Worn every year. Pinned just so."

He didn't look at the crowd.

He looked at Agnes.

Then at the crown.

Then at the shawl.

"And she never sat outside this long. Not in winter. Not with her joints."

Annabel glanced sideways at him.

"You think something is wrong."

He didn't answer immediately.

Persephone blinked.

Then Benedict said, softly:

"I think people want her death to make sense.

And I think Agnes wouldn't have made it easy."

Chapter 3

The chapel smelled of beeswax and cold lilies.

Not the comforting kind—*the kind that meant something had ended.*

Barbara Ellington sat at the long oak table with her pen poised like a sceptre. Her planner was open, her scarf tucked just-so into her tailored coat, and a small plate of untouched shortbread sat between her and the vicar.

"We'll hold the funeral in three days," she said firmly. "That gives everyone time to prepare."

Across from her, Reverend Harrow folded his hands and said nothing. His eyebrows twitched in mild protest, but he didn't speak.

Annabel sat near the end of the table, one hand around a mug of tea gone cold. Evie stood by the door, arms crossed, coat still on, clearly resisting the urge to flee.

"I just think," Annabel said gently, "we should be sure Agnes would've wanted it that soon."

Barbara smiled without warmth.

"Annabel dear, no one knows Agnes's wishes better than the community."

"Except Agnes," Evie muttered.

Barbara ignored her. She turned a page in her planner with the crispness of someone handling something fragile but tiresome.

"She had no close family. No will on record. And she would've wanted the Procession to go ahead. She told me as much last year — 'Tradition above all.' Those were her exact words."

"Are you sure she meant *this* tradition?" Annabel asked.

The room went still for half a breath.

Barbara straightened her back.

"Agnes was the Spirit of the Season for nearly four decades. She was Little Firling's heart. And hearts deserve ceremony, not speculation."

"No one's speculating," said Evie.

"We just—don't know everything yet."

"We rarely do," the vicar said quietly. "But we honour what we can."

Barbara smiled at him like he was a small dog who had barked politely.

"We'll have candlelight, seasonal hymns, a reading from her favourite carol—"

"Which one was that?" Evie asked.

"Well, I—she—*Silent Night,* I believe."

"She hated *Silent Night,*" muttered Annabel.

Persephone, who had slipped in unnoticed, leapt onto the windowsill behind them and knocked over a pot of dried holly. No one moved to stop her.

"We'll also dedicate the Procession to her," Barbara continued, dabbing a speck of dust off her coat. "A single candle will be carried in her place. Symbolic. Poetic. Healing."

Annabel looked at the mistletoe crown on the side table.

It still sat where it had been left. One ribbon trailing. One sprig missing.

She couldn't look away from it.

***

The wind outside the chapel had teeth.

Annabel wrapped her scarf tighter as she stepped down the path. Evie walked beside her, hands shoved into coat pockets, muttering something under her breath that might've been about bureaucracy or hymns or both.

They didn't speak for a moment.

The sky was the colour of unpolished pewter, and the snow that had started the day before had turned into a thin, slushy mess that clung to boots and bad moods.

"Three days," Evie finally said.

"Because nothing says respect like rushing someone into the ground."

"It's not disrespect," Annabel said softly. "It's fear. No one wants to sit in the waiting."

"Yeah, well. They should try it sometime. Builds character."

They passed the chapel's side garden, where yesterday's flowers had already begun to wilt in the frost. The mistletoe crown sat inside the chapel on the windowsill, behind the glass. It looked smaller somehow. Or just lonelier.

"You're thinking about the crown again," Evie said.

Annabel didn't answer.

Because she was.

Because *something was wrong.*

***

They reached the edge of the green just as Nora was locking up the bookshop, balancing a paper bag full of clementines and a small stack of hymnbooks under one arm.

"You two look like someone fed you figgy pudding too early," she said, cheerful but tired.

"We just came from the planning meeting," Annabel replied.

"Ah. That'll do it."

Nora glanced toward the chapel. Her expression softened.

"Barbara means well, but she forgets people are people before they're legacies."

"She said Agnes wanted the Procession to go on," Evie said. "That it was her final wish."

Nora gave a small laugh, not cruel, just... amused.

"Agnes told me last week she thought the whole thing was getting too big. Said it had lost its heart."

Annabel blinked.

"She said that?"

"Mm-hmm. And that if anyone tried to turn her funeral into a publicity photo, she'd come back and haunt them. Quietly. With drafts."

Evie snorted.

Annabel didn't.

"Why would Barbara lie?" she asked.

"Barbara doesn't lie," Nora said. "She just remembers things the way she wants to."

Persephone appeared from behind a post-box, tail high, fur flecked with frost.

She walked between them without a sound, then sat.

And stared at the chapel.

Like it had just told her something no one else was listening to.

***

They were halfway across the square when the voice stopped them.

"She hated Silent Night."

Annabel turned first.

Grace stood beneath the lantern by the bakery, coat buttoned to the neck, hands tucked into the sleeves like they didn't quite belong to her.

She didn't move closer.

Didn't blink much either.

"She said it felt like the end of something instead of a beginning."

Evie raised an eyebrow.

Annabel blinked.

"Were you at the meeting?" she asked.

Grace shook her head.

"Didn't need to be. I knew what they'd say."

She looked past them, toward the chapel.

Then added, almost too softly to hear:

"They don't know her."

"And you did?" Evie asked, careful but sharp.

Grace didn't answer that.

She just looked at Annabel.

And said:

"She wouldn't have gone outside without her shawl."

Then she walked away.

Not fast.

Just like someone *who didn't need to stay to be sure she'd been heard.*

***

Evie waited until Grace had disappeared past the bakery.

"Who *is* she?" she asked, low.

Annabel exhaled.

"I don't know. She was at the rehearsal. Quiet. Watching Agnes the whole time."

"People watch Agnes all the time. Doesn't mean they *know* her."

Evie kicked a patch of snow with slightly more aggression than necessary.

"You don't just walk up, drop a fact like that, and then disappear like some tragic snow fairy."

Annabel didn't answer. She was still thinking about the mistletoe crown. About the missing sprig.

And now... the shawl.

***

The warmth hit them in a wave of lavender, woodsmoke, and the faint trace of burnt toast Evie had caused that morning on entering Honeystone cottage.

Annabel set the crown gently on the kitchen table.

"If it were crushed," she said, "we could blame the fall. But it's not. And it wasn't on her head."

"I still think it looks cursed," Evie muttered, pulling off her boots. "But I've got the investigative instincts of a sledgehammer."

Annabel leaned in, running her fingers along the woven frame.

One ribbon frayed.

One mistletoe sprig broken—*not snapped*, but *twisted*.

Not fallen off.

Removed?

She didn't say it aloud.

But Persephone jumped onto the windowsill, stretched... and hopped down.

With absolute intent.

"If you knock it off the table, I swear—" Evie started.

But Persephone didn't go for the crown.

She walked to the little sideboard near the back window, sniffed...

...then stuck one paw under the edge.

A crinkle.

A gentle, papery rustle.

Annabel opened the drawer.

Inside, between a stack of unused napkins and a birthday candle shaped like the number seven—

A folded envelope.

Not theirs.

"That wasn't there this morning," Annabel whispered.

Evie raised an eyebrow.

"You sure Persephone didn't forge it? Seems to be taking a lead on this one."

***

Annabel held the envelope like it might crumble if she breathed too hard.

It was soft from handling. Not new.

The edges were slightly smudged with what might've been flour, or chalk, or the kind of dust only old stories leave behind.

Her name wasn't on it.

There was no address.

Just a small flourish across the centre of the envelope.

"To be given only if she asked."

Evie leaned in.

"Oh, that's not ominous at all."

"It's Agnes's handwriting," Annabel whispered.

She opened it carefully.

Inside was a single sheet, folded in half, no creases but the one down the middle. No dates. Just... words.

Neat. Measured. Meant.

She read aloud.

"If this finds you, it means I couldn't bring myself to ask her. And that's my fault.

There are things I left unsaid. And someone still might come looking for the truth.

If she does... be kind. She's more tangled in this than she realises.

And remind her—people can love more than one way.

Just not always at the same time."

The silence that followed felt heavier than the snow outside.

Annabel refolded the letter carefully and placed it on the kitchen table beside the mistletoe crown.

Evie poured tea into two mismatched mugs and set one down with a thunk.

"So," she said, dropping into the chair across from her, "we think shawl-girl is the mystery woman from the letter?"

Annabel stared at the fire for a moment.

"We don't *know* that."

"No, but you *want* to."

"I just..."

She exhaled.

"She watched Agnes like she knew her. She knew about Silent Night. And the shawl. And the way she said it—like it wasn't just an observation. Like it *hurt.*"

Evie sipped her tea and winced slightly.

Too hot.

"Could've been a fluke. Or she was close with someone else who knew Agnes. There are people in this village with opinions about Agnes who couldn't pick her out of a line-up of stained-glass saints."

"But the letter said *she* might come looking," Annabel murmured.

"And if she does—be kind."

Evie looked up.

"You think she's Agnes's—what? Granddaughter? Secret mentee? Illegitimate time-travelling daughter?"

"I don't know. But she wasn't just...
there. She was *watching. Waiting.* And
now she's grieving like someone who
missed her chance."

Evie leaned back and stared at the
ceiling.

"Okay. Let's say you're right.

She's connected. She was meant to
hear the truth.

That still doesn't mean she's telling
us everything."

Annabel looked down at the letter
again.

Her fingertips brushed the edge of
the paper like it might still be warm.

"If she was part of the truth Agnes
never said...

then maybe the person who did this didn't want her to find it."

***

The fire crackled.

The letter lay between the mugs.

The mistletoe crown sat on a folded tea towel—fragile, uneven, slightly sagging to one side like it had lost its centre of gravity.

Persephone had been perched on the windowsill the whole time. Watching.

Judging.

Plotting, probably.

Now she leapt down with a soft thud and trotted across the floor with that signature blend of *elegance and menace.*

Evie side-eyed her.

"If she knocks that crown off the table again, I'm staging a mutiny."

But Persephone didn't knock.

She circled the table.

Sniffed the crown once.

Then very gently batted the ribbon at its base. Not playfully. *With intent.*

The broken mistletoe sprig—*still tucked loosely into the frame*—shifted.

Annabel leaned in.

"Wait—"

She reached out and carefully lifted the sprig out of its woven loop.

The end of it wasn't just twisted.

It was...

Clean. Snapped deliberately.

And—

There was something tucked inside the tiny knot of ribbon.

A *slip of paper.*

Folded. Tiny. Hidden deep.

Evie looked like she was watching a magician pull doves out of tea towels.

"Okay, why does this crown have *subplots?*"

Annabel unfolded the scrap slowly.

It wasn't a letter.

Just a single line. Written in what looked like charcoal pencil.

"Some things only bloom once."

Chapter 4

Grace hadn't meant to walk to the edge of the green again.

Her boots made no sound on the snow, and her hands had gone cold long ago, but she didn't move faster. There wasn't anywhere else she needed to be.

She didn't stay at the inn. Too many questions. Too many eyes.

Instead, she'd found a small flat above the flower shop, let out over winter by a woman who'd gone to stay with her son in Devon. The window overlooked the square.

From there, she could see the chapel.

And the bench where they'd found her.

Agnes.

She still couldn't say the name out loud.

Not like her father had.

***

She'd grown up hearing pieces of Agnes Thorne in the way some children heard fairy tales.

Not full stories—just *gestures.*

A name spoken too gently.

A silence after a certain song.

The way her father looked at old photographs like he'd lost something the picture couldn't hold.

"She made the world feel softer," he'd once said.

"But only if you let it."

Grace hadn't asked what he meant.

She always meant to.

He died before she could.

***

Now she was here, in a village that looked like a postcard, *watching grief move like fog through cobblestone streets.*

They didn't know her.

Some looked kindly.

Some looked curious.

Some didn't look at all.

And then there were the two women from the rehearsal.

The ones who saw her see Agnes.

She hadn't meant to speak.

The words just came.

"She hated Silent Night."

She didn't even know how she remembered that.

She only knew it had been true.

***

She sat now by the window, a mug of tea cooling beside her, untouched.

She'd unpacked nothing.

The one letter she'd brought—*her father's*—stayed folded in her coat pocket. Still unread.

She couldn't bring herself to look at it.

Not yet.

Not without... *something.*

***

A knock at the door broke the stillness.

Not loud.

Just... steady.

Like someone had been waiting for the right moment to ask a question.

She didn't move at first.

But then she did.

Because something in her had already decided:

If they're here for answers…

I hope they understand I don't have them all.

***

Grace remembered that he'd been tired that day.

That kind of tired that sits behind the eyes and doesn't ask for sympathy— just silence.

Grace had come home early.

She didn't know why.

She just... did.

He sat in his armchair by the window, a worn book resting on his knee, though he hadn't turned the page in ages.

"You okay, Dad?"

He smiled.

"Just visiting the past. It always borrows more time than I think."

She crouched beside him.

The light through the window cast soft amber lines across the side of his face.

"Who were you thinking about?"

He didn't answer immediately.

Then he reached for the envelope on the table.

The handwriting was careful.

"I never gave her this," he said.

"I wrote it. Packed it. Rehearsed every word.

Then I didn't go."

"Why?"

"Because I thought there'd be time."

A pause.

Then, quieter:

"*Some things... only bloom once.*"

***

The knock came again.

Grace stood just behind the door; breath held like it might change the outcome.

She already knew who it was.

She didn't know what they'd ask.

She opened it.

Annabel stood on the step, coat dusted with frost, her eyes soft and searching. Beside her, Evie hovered like a backup generator — warm and necessary, if occasionally sparking.

Persephone wasn't with them.

And that was somehow worse.

Annabel didn't speak at first.

She just lifted the mistletoe crown — wrapped gently in a scarf, cradled like something sacred and fragile and still waiting.

"We found something," she said.

Grace looked at the crown.

At the broken sprig.

At the ribbon.

At the space where something had once been.

"I don't know what you think I—"

"The message was hidden in the crown," Annabel said gently.

"It said: *Some things only bloom once.*"

Grace's breath hitched.

She didn't blink.

She just stood there, perfectly still, as if one wrong movement might unravel her entirely.

"He said that," she whispered.

"My dad. Before he died."

Evie shifted beside her.

"Did he say... who he meant?"

Grace shook her head.

"He never told me her name.

Just that there was someone.

And that he never sent the letter."

Annabel glanced at Evie.

Then back at Grace.

"Agnes left us something.

A letter.

It was meant to be given… *if she never found the courage to ask you herself.*"

Grace didn't speak.

She looked at the crown again.

And this time, she stepped back from the doorway.

Just far enough to let them in.

***

They didn't go far—just to the little sitting room that smelled faintly of forgotten tulips and worn paper.

Annabel unwrapped the crown and set it gently on the coffee table. She placed the folded letter beside it. Pale envelope. No name.

Grace stared at it like it might vanish if she looked too hard.

Evie sat on the arm of the couch; arms crossed but softer than usual.

Persephone had slipped in, unnoticed, and curled in the corner chair like a guardian who didn't believe in explanations.

Grace reached for the letter. Her fingers trembled, but she didn't stop.

She opened it. And read.

***

Grace—

I was never brave in the way your father deserved.

He offered me something quiet and true, and I gave him excuses dressed as reasons.

I thought I'd have time. We both did.

But time is cruel to those who wait.

If you've come to Little Firling, then maybe he's gone. And maybe you're looking for answers I never had the courage to offer.

You don't owe me anything.

But I owe you this:

You were wanted. You were dreamed about. And whatever you've been told, I hope you know—

some things bloom once, and never stop echoing.

If I'm not here to tell you this, then I was too late.

And I'm sorry.

***

Grace didn't cry.

She just folded the letter again, slowly, like something sacred.

Her voice was a thread of frost and breath.

"He told me he wrote to someone. That he never sent it."

She looked up.

"He loved her. But he wouldn't say her name.

Just that... he failed her.

And she never came back."

Annabel leaned forward, elbows on knees.

"He never stopped waiting, did he?"

Grace shook her head.

Evie, unusually quiet, uncrossed her arms.

"She never stopped remembering either. That letter... it's not guilt. It's grief."

Grace blinked.

For a moment, the silence was warm.

"He used to say... some people arrive like spring.

And some like winter.

But Agnes... was both."

***

The fire had burned low, casting soft amber ribbons across the table.

Persephone shifted slightly in her sleep, tail twitching like she was listening even with her eyes closed.

Grace traced the edge of her tea mug.

"He never remarried," she said softly.

"Said no one else ever made the world feel... less lonely."

Annabel nodded.

"Agnes never spoke of him. Not out loud.

But she had a way of pausing whenever someone mentioned the years before she came to Little Firling."

She smiled faintly.

"Like she was holding her breath under a memory."

Grace looked down at the letter in her hands.

"He taught me to plant things.

We didn't have a garden, but he'd grow tomatoes on the windowsill.

Said *'You never know what'll bloom if you just give it the chance.'*

Evie tilted her head.

"Agnes always said that exact thing. About the children she mentored.

About the Snowdrop Circle."

For a moment, the room was quiet in the *best way.*

Not full of tension.

Just full of *stories finally speaking to each other.*

***

Annabel leaned forward.

"Do you want to stay? For the funeral?"

Grace hesitated.

"I don't know.

I didn't come for closure.

I came because something in me said *go.*

Now I'm here and..."

She looked at the crown.

"I feel like something's still unfinished."

Evie spoke, low and careful.

"It might be."

***

Outside, beneath the frost-dusted hedge

A figure stood in the narrow alley beside the flower shop, where lamplight didn't quite reach.

They watched the glow of the flat upstairs.

Saw the flicker of shadows moving inside.

They didn't move.

Didn't speak.

Just stood.

Still.

Waiting.

Like someone who thought *they'd buried the past long ago...*

...and was *terrified to see it blooming*

again.

Chapter 5

The next morning smelled like frost and regret.

Annabel was just unlocking the garden gate when Benedict Harper appeared, scarf tucked, gloves on, and the kind of face that suggested he'd already finished the newspaper *and* reorganised a cupboard before 8 a.m.

"You're up early," she said, managing a tired smile.

"Didn't sleep," he replied.

He held something small in his gloved hand—a weathered paperback, spine cracked but well-kept.

"Agnes lent this to me," he said, offering it. "Said I'd enjoy it. I did. But it wasn't really about the book."

Annabel tilted her head.

"What was it about?"

Benedict looked past her, toward the garden.

His voice lowered.

"She asked me once…"

"Do you think it's possible to regret something more as you get older, not less?"

Annabel's heart thudded gently.

"She didn't say what she meant?"

"No," he said softly.

"But she was holding this book.

And she was crying, though she didn't realise it until I offered her a tissue."

He paused.

Then added, almost too lightly:

"She never did tell me what it was she lost.

But it wasn't a thing.

It was a person."

***

The watcher stood beside the fence behind the bakery, hidden just enough to blend with morning deliveries and wheelbarrow ruts.

They'd followed Benedict since sunrise.

Not close.

Not daring.

Just... *present.*

And now they heard it.

The name.

The memory.

The word "lost."

A tremor flickered across their face.

And then—

The smallest smile.

Not warm.

Not cruel.

Just... *resigned.*

The kind of smile that says:

They're catching up.

But they still don't know what matters most.

Not yet.

***

Grace didn't sleep much.

The flat above the flower shop was quiet enough—just the creak of old pipes and the occasional rattle of wind against the pane—but her thoughts made too much noise.

She'd reread the letter three times.

Then folded it.

Then unfolded it again.

She didn't cry.

Not because it didn't hurt.

But because *it had been hurting for years, quietly, without a name.*

***

She sat at the small table by the window; hands curled around a mug gone cold hours ago.

The chapel was just visible through the trees.

So was the bench.

She didn't look at it directly.

Instead, she looked at the envelope still tucked in her coat pocket.

Not Agnes's.

Her father's.

Still sealed.

Still untouched.

She ran her thumb across the edge.

Just open it, she thought.

But she didn't.

Because if Agnes's letter had *confirmed everything that she feared...*

Then this one might *undo it.*

Or worse—

Make it more complicated.

***

There was something else, too.

A whisper in the back of her mind.

Not from the letter.

From the chapel.

Something about the way Agnes had looked that day.

The way she'd been sitting.

The shawl on the steps.

Grace's father had taught her how to spot things that didn't belong—*when stories didn't quite match.*

And this story?

It *felt too tidy.*

***

Grace stood up, slowly.

She didn't know what she was going to do next.

But she knew this:

"If someone thought this was finished...

They didn't know her at all."

***

Grace had wandered to the bakery without meaning to.

The smell of cinnamon and butter curled around the doorway like an old friend she hadn't seen since childhood.

She wasn't hungry.

But she stepped inside anyway.

Inside, Rosie's mum—Mira—was pulling trays from the oven, face flushed, apron dusted with flour and sugar and something cheerier than grief.

"Morning, love," Mira said kindly. "Haven't seen you in a bit."

"Didn't plan on being seen," Grace replied with a small smile.

Mira offered a biscuit without asking.

"For warmth, not comfort. Let's not pretend sugar fixes everything."

Grace took it.

Sat on the stool near the counter.

Mira kept working, voice light, movements rhythmic.

"Rosie's been asking about Agnes every night," she said softly. "Keeps saying she saw her *looking up at the sky.*"

"Said she was smiling. But Rosie doesn't know what fear looks like yet."

Grace blinked. "Smiling?"

"Yeah. Little half-smile." Mira shook her head.

"But that's the thing—when we found her, her mouth wasn't smiling at all.

It was..."

She hesitated.

"It was still. Flat. Too still."

She tossed a cloth over the tray.

"But you know kids. They fill in blanks with the softest things they can imagine."

Grace didn't respond.

Because *she remembered* Agnes at the rehearsal.

And *Agnes hadn't looked up once.*

***

Persephone moved through the back garden like mist.

Annabel had left the door cracked open. Just enough.

The wind carried no scent of baking.

No smoke.

Only frost and old things.

She walked along the garden path.

Paused near the rosebush.

Sniffed.

Then veered sharply—toward the low stone wall.

Toward the hedgerow.

She stopped.

Sat.

Stared at a patch of disturbed snow.

Not much.

Just enough for someone small to miss.

Or someone clever to notice.

She blinked slowly.

Then stood.

And with the slow, deliberate grace of someone who already knows the ending—

She walked away.

Chapter 6

It was late afternoon when Annabel knelt in the garden, gloves damp, breath fogging gently as the last light slid between the trees.

Evie stood a few feet away, eyeing a patch of disturbed snow Persephone had circled earlier.

"You're really trusting the cat now?" Evie asked, one brow raised.

"She's smarter than us and you know it."

Evie crouched beside her. "Looks like someone stepped here. Recently."

The snow had melted in a small crescent, like something had knelt—or crouched—and disturbed the surface. Beneath it, a faint line of dark soil showed.

Annabel gently pulled her trowel from the basket and began clearing around the area. She didn't expect to find anything. But then...

"Evie."

She said it so softly that Evie leaned in on instinct. Annabel brushed aside another clump of earth.

There, tucked just beneath the surface—

Was a *flower bulb*.

Not a rare one. A snowdrop.

But *out of season*.

And *wrapped in muslin*.

Evie frowned.

"That's not natural planting."

"No," Annabel whispered.

"It's a message."

The muslin had faint markings. Ink blurred by moisture.

But one word was still visible.

"Bloom."

***

Annabel and Evie were just closing the back gate when Grace appeared—coat buttoned, scarf too loose, cheeks pink with cold and something like urgency.

"I didn't mean to interrupt," she said. "But I—something doesn't feel right."

Evie shot Annabel a look that said: *This feels familiar.*

"Come in," Annabel said gently.

"We've just found something ourselves."

***

Inside Honeystone Cottage, the kettle sang quietly, Persephone circled Grace once like a living question mark, and the snowdrop bulb sat on the counter, still half-wrapped in muslin.

Grace looked at it and blinked.

"Snowdrop."

"Yes," Annabel said. "Buried outside the house. Recently. Wrapped. Marked."

Evie pointed to the muslin.

"One word left on it. 'Bloom.'"

Grace exhaled—too slowly.

"That word again."

Annabel leaned forward slightly.

"You've heard it before?"

"He said it. My dad. Whenever he spoke about her—Agnes—he'd say things like *she made things bloom just by believing they could.*"

"And the letter—Agnes's letter—used it too," Annabel murmured.

"*Some things only bloom once,*" Grace echoed.

She sat down slowly. Like she was placing her thoughts down before they scattered.

"There's something else."

Evie crossed her arms. Carefully.

"What is it?"

"I ran into Rosie's mum. She said Rosie told her Agnes was *smiling*—looking up at the sky.

But when they found her... she wasn't."

The room went still.

Even Persephone sat straighter.

Annabel looked at the snowdrop again.

"She wasn't smiling. That's been said again and again.

She looked... still. Cold. Too cold."

Evie frowned.

"Unless she was moved."

Silence.

Then Grace whispered:

"Or unless Rosie saw her *before* it happened."

Chapter 7

Annabel unrolled the butcher paper she kept near the pantry—usually for wrapping vegetables, but now for *truths.*

She flattened it on the table, weighed it down with a salt shaker and a jam jar, and drew a clean line through the middle.

"Let's just look at what we know," she said quietly. "No speculation. Just time."

Evie grabbed a pencil and leaned in.

"Rehearsal ended at 5:15 sharp. Barbara announced the end like she was releasing doves."

"And Agnes left through the side chapel door," Grace added. "I saw her go. Alone."

Annabel marked that down.

"Rosie and her parents found her around 6 p.m."

"Fifty minutes," Evie said. "Give or take."

"But Rosie said she saw her *smiling*, looking at the sky. That doesn't match what her mum saw. Or what *we* saw."

Grace leaned in.

"If Rosie saw her *before* she froze... then she saw her while Agnes was still alive."

Evie drummed her fingers.

"So, either Agnes was sitting outside, in the cold, willingly... for nearly an hour—without her shawl—"

"—Which she never would've done," Annabel cut in.

"—Or someone moved her there."

Grace whispered:

"Or she met someone before she ever made it home."

The room fell quiet.

Outside, the snow began again.

Soft. Deceptive.

***

Annabel circled a small gap on the timeline.

"This is what we don't know," she said.

"Where was Agnes between 5:15 and 6:00 p.m.?

And *who* was with her?"

Evie's voice dropped.

"And *what* happened during that time... that no one wants to say out loud?"

***

They were walking home from the chapel when Grace stopped short.

Annabel turned.

"Are you okay?"

Grace didn't answer.

Her gaze fixed on the side door—the one barely used by anyone but Agnes, the one Rosie's mother said was found unlatched that day.

She stared at it for a moment longer, then walked toward it slowly, boots crunching softly over patchy snow and frozen grass.

She reached out.

Touched the handle.

Closed her eyes.

"It slammed."

Annabel blinked.

"What did?"

"The door," Grace whispered.

"That day. At the end of the rehearsal."

She opened her eyes.

"I didn't see her. Not clearly. I just heard the door shut. And I saw... movement. A coat.

I thought—"

Her voice cracked like thawing ice.

"I thought it was her."

Evie, a few steps behind, frowned.

"What colour?"

Grace looked back at her.

"Dark blue. Maybe navy. With red or burgundy at the cuff."

Evie looked at Annabel.

"That's not what she was wearing when they found her.

Agnes had her green wool coat on. The same one she's worn since forever."

Grace whispered:

"Then it wasn't her I saw."

Chapter 8

Persephone had not followed them into the chapel. She had her own investigation.

The side door—old wood, cold to the touch—creaked in the wind, just slightly ajar.

Persephone didn't meow.

She didn't sniff the air like other cats might.

She stepped into the ivy-wrapped edge of the chapel wall and stared.

Still. Waiting.

Then—without hesitation—she slipped into the frozen tangle at the base of the wall.

A rustle.

A pause.

She emerged a moment later, tail flicking in satisfaction.

In her mouth, a small object gleamed softly against the frost.

***

Annabel spotted her first.

"Persephone—what have you—oh."

Evie crouched.

"That's a button."

It was round, brass-edged, dark navy in the centre.

And just visible—on the rim—was a tiny embroidered thread of burgundy.

Annabel touched it with gloved fingers.

"That's not Agnes's."

Grace's voice came from behind them. Quiet. Certain.

"That's from the coat I saw."

***

Benedict arrived with his usual punctuality and a brown paper bag filled with three scones and the kind of calm that felt handwoven.

Annabel met him at the front gate.

"You've brought backup carbs," Evie said as he stepped inside.

"Mystery burns calories," he replied, with a slight smile.

But his tone was more subdued than usual.

He sat, hands resting on the table, his gaze lingering not on the food... but on the snowdrop bulb still nestled in its tea towel.

"I heard you found something."

"A button," Annabel said. "Persephone retrieved it."

"And we think someone left through the side chapel door," Grace added.

Benedict paused.

"The side door?"

Benedict paused, teacup still in hand.

"She asked me to oil the side door two weeks ago," he said quietly.

"Said she didn't want it creaking. Not during rehearsals. Said it made her feel like she was being followed."

He chuckled faintly.

"I thought she was just being poetic."

Evie's eyes didn't leave his face.

"Or maybe... she wasn't."

Benedict looked up.

"Pardon?"

"Maybe she wasn't worried about the creak.

Maybe she thought someone was following her."

The room went still.

Even Persephone lifted her head, tail curling around her paws like punctuation.

Benedict swallowed.

Something fragile flickered across his face.

"I didn't think…"

"She didn't say—"

He stopped himself.

Annabel watched him closely.

"But she said something," she said softly. "Enough that it stayed with you."

He nodded once.

"She didn't ask me to fix things often."

Chapter 9

They'd stepped into the square for air.

Too much tea. Too many theories.

Even Persephone needed a break from all the quiet tension.

Annabel, Evie, and Grace walked slowly past the noticeboard outside the chapel, frost crackling gently beneath their boots.

That's when they saw her.

Gillian Berridge — the choir organiser, carol vigilante, and lifelong soprano wrangler — was pinning up the rehearsal list with military precision and a deeply unimpressed frown.

"Afternoon," Annabel offered.

"Oh, there you are," Gillian replied without looking up.

"I was just thinking about Agnes and that business with the side door.

Terrible, isn't it? Terrible."

Evie leaned in just slightly, tone casual.

"We're still trying to piece it together.

But someone left something behind."

Gillian's fingers paused mid-pin.

"Oh?"

"A button," Evie said. "Navy, brass-edged. Burgundy thread. Pretty distinctive."

Gillian went still.

Just for a moment.

"That sounds familiar..." she said at last.

"There was someone—joined the choir a few years ago.

Had a coat like that. Reminded me of something from a boarding school. Wool, but formal. Almost theatrical."

"Do you remember who it was?" Grace asked gently.

Gillian blinked.

Too fast.

"No. I... no. I must be misremembering.

People come and go. Especially in December."

She turned back to the noticeboard.

"If I think of anything, I'll let you know."

She left the last pin crooked.

And walked away a little too quickly, leaving the corner of the carol sheet fluttering in the wind.

***

They'd taken the long way around the chapel—Persephone trailing behind like she had somewhere better to be and wasn't telling them what it was.

Annabel paused near the old side door.

It was tucked in an alcove of ivy-covered stone, half-hidden behind a crooked rain barrel and a collection of donation baskets currently catching dead leaves.

She reached out, gloved fingers brushing the handle.

She didn't turn it with urgency—just curiosity.

Memory.

Instinct.

It didn't move.

Locked.

Evie caught up, boots crunching behind her.

"Stuck?"

"No," Annabel said softly. "Locked."

She stepped back, brow furrowed slightly.

"You need a key from the outside. But from inside..." she trailed off.

"You can open it freely."

Evie looked at the worn iron and flaking paint.

"So, whoever used it... was either already inside—or had the key."

They exchanged a glance.

Annabel didn't say it out loud.

But the question hung there anyway.

Who still has a key to the door Agnes didn't trust?

Chapter 10

The vicar, Reverend Harrow, was leaning over a stack of tattered hymnals when Annabel and Evie found him.

The chapel was quiet, sunlight cutting across the wooden pews in pale gold strips. A few leftover holly leaves still clung to the window ledge.

He straightened, smiling politely beneath wire-rimmed glasses.

"Ladies. Was the carol list too sharp for some ears already?"

Evie grinned.

"We're not here about music."

"Pity. I had my best alto complaint face ready."

Annabel stepped forward gently.

"We're asking about the side door."

The vicar blinked.

"The south vestibule?"

"The one that stays locked," she clarified. "Unless someone has a key."

"Ah." His tone changed, just slightly. Still warm. But guarded.

"Not many do. We don't use it much."

"Who *does* have one?" Evie asked.

Reverend Harrow folded his hands.

"Myself, of course. Gillian Berridge, for choir access.

Nathan, our groundskeeper—though he rarely uses it.

And until recently... Agnes."

Annabel exchanged a look with Evie.

"Anyone else?"

A pause. "The mayor's wife had one. Years ago. I believe it was returned."

"Believe?"

"She's not a woman one presses about sacred things," he said with a faint smile.

But then—

"There might be one more floating about.

One was misplaced during the roof repairs in 2021.

We changed the locks after, but—"

He trailed off.

"Agnes didn't want a new key. Said the old one suited her just fine."

***

The parish hall smelled of furniture polish, boiled tea, and cautious condolences.

A folding table had been dragged beneath the window, now surrounded by a patchwork of chairs filled with Little Firling's most committed doers — the ones who arranged flowers before services and formed strategic carol committees behind the vicar's back.

Annabel and Evie slipped in quietly.

At the head of the table sat Barbara Ellington, the mayor's wife, chin lifted, pearls clicking gently as she tapped a pen against her notepad.

"We must make this respectful but not maudlin," she announced.

"Agnes hated fuss."

Gillian Berridge sat three chairs down, flipping through hymn options and correcting spellings that didn't exist.

Nathan, the groundskeeper, leaned on the back of a chair, dirt still under his nails.

Reverend Harrow stood, arms folded, the only one not pretending this wasn't uncomfortable.

"Do we have someone to speak for her?" he asked gently.

"Family?"

The silence that followed was so awkward it almost clanged.

"She was... part of all of us," Barbara said, with the kind of tone that meant *don't argue or I'll host the wake myself.*

*****

Then came the moment—

Annabel was scribbling flower notes beside Gillian when she glanced across the table.

Nathan had just been asked about chapel access for casket delivery.

"You'll have the keys, yes?" Barbara asked.

He nodded.

"Aye, the front and vestry."

Barbara hesitated.

"You'll need the side door, too. For the pallbearers."

Nathan's brow furrowed.

"Didn't think I still had that one. Haven't used it in months."

Annabel's head lifted.

"You don't still, have it?"

"Should be in the maintenance box, maybe?" he said uncertainly.

"Could check."

Gillian cleared her throat.

"I returned mine. Gave it back to Agnes at Easter."

Annabel's pen stilled.

Evie didn't look up, but her hand curled tighter around her tea.

Reverend Harrow raised an eyebrow.

"That's... interesting. She didn't mention that."

"Well, I'm sure she forgot," Gillian said smoothly.

"We were both terribly busy with the spring concert."

Chapter 11

They were walking home when it started to snow again.

Not much. Just a slow drift, the kind that whispered rather than fell.

Persephone padded ahead, tail high, unconcerned.

Evie broke the silence first.

"Three keys."

Annabel didn't pretend not to know what she meant.

"Five," she said quietly.

Evie squinted at her.

"Wait—five?"

"Harrow. Nathan. Gillian. Barbara Ellington's, if she really returned it. And the one that vanished during the 2021 roof repairs."

Evie groaned.

"Right. So, five keys. One door. One dead woman."

"And one very good liar," Annabel murmured.

They walked a few more steps in silence.

Then Annabel added, more to herself than to Evie—

"She didn't leave that way."

"What?"

"Agnes. The way they found her. Out on the stone steps.

She didn't walk out there.

Not in that cold. Not without her shawl.

She didn't go willingly."

Evie was quiet.

Then—

"So, someone else did."

Annabel nodded once.

"And someone used a key to do it."

***

They'd just reached the corner by the chapel wall when Grace stepped out from the narrow footpath, arms folded, scarf tucked too tightly, expression unreadable.

Persephone meowed once — not annoyed, not welcoming. Just... acknowledging.

"You two always this quiet when you're walking?" Grace asked.

Annabel blinked.

Evie recovered faster.

"Only when we're accidentally solving things."

"You're not just walking," Grace said flatly.

"Not exactly," Annabel admitted.

Grace glanced between them, eyes narrowing just a fraction.

"You've found something. Or... someone said something."

She looked at Annabel now, more directly.

"What is it?"

Annabel hesitated.

Evie didn't.

"Keys."

Grace tilted her head.

"To what?"

"To the side chapel door," Evie said. "The one Agnes never used. Until she did."

Grace went still.

"That door was locked."

"Exactly," Annabel said. "And only a few people ever had the key.

Except now... no one seems to know where their copy is. Or if they ever returned it.

One was lost during repairs.

One was supposedly handed back to Agnes.

One's 'probably' in a tool box."

"And one," Evie added, "belonged to Barbara Ellington.

But apparently that key just evaporated after she got promoted to Mayor's Wife."

Grace was quiet for a long time.

Then she said, so softly they almost missed it—

"Agnes told me once... that she didn't like the sound that door made.

Said it felt like someone breathing behind her."

Annabel turned slowly.

"She said that to you?"

Grace nodded.

"Last month. After rehearsal.

She looked... rattled. But she laughed it off."

Evie exhaled.

"That's not the sound of a woman just worried about hinges."

***

The chapel was quiet.

Not funeral quiet. Not reverent.

Just still, in the way old stone buildings go when they've heard enough prayers and not quite enough truth.

Persephone padded in before the humans did.

She didn't pause at the altar.

Didn't flinch at the side door.

Didn't blink at the scent of polish and petals.

She went straight for the front right pew.

The one Agnes always chose when she wasn't standing, conducting, correcting.

Annabel followed her gaze, a half-step behind.

"That was her spot," she whispered.

Persephone hopped up—graceful, silent—then turned once in a circle before pressing her paw into the corner of the seat cushion.

It shifted.

Evie was there in an instant, lifting the edge.

Underneath—tucked barely under the edge of the fabric—

Was a *folded scrap of thick paper.*

Torn from a choir programme.

Faint pencil scrawl across the back.

Annabel took it carefully.

Three words.

"She used mine."

***

Annabel stared at the paper, thumb brushing the edge.

Annabel stared at the paper, thumb brushing the edge.

Evie leaned in, squinting.

"That's her handwriting," she said softly.

"The way she curls her s's. Always tilted forward. Like she's leaning into everything she says."

Grace read the words aloud.

"She used mine."

Evie spoke slowly, carefully.

"She's not talking about a copy. She means someone used *her* key.

Not theirs. Not one they claimed they gave back.

Someone came through that door.

And she *knew* who it was."

"She wrote this," Annabel whispered, "right before she died."

Grace's breath caught.

"The pew cushions... they were only brought back that morning.

She joked about it. Said she'd finally be able to sit through a rehearsal without bruises."

Evie closed her eyes for a second.

"She saw them come in."

"And she didn't have time to run," Grace said.

Annabel swallowed.

"But she had time to leave this."

Persephone nestled into the pew, tail curling like punctuation, body pressed against the silence.

The chapel was still.

But something beneath the quiet had cracked open.

Chapter 12

They didn't speak much after they left the chapel.

Even Evie had gone quiet, her hands stuffed deep in her coat pockets, eyes scanning the pavement like it might offer something else they missed.

Persephone walked between them, tail flicking against the wind. She didn't look back once.

Grace broke the silence first. "She knew."

No one disagreed.

"She knew someone had her key," Grace continued.

"She knew they were coming through the door.

And she knew they were coming for her."

Evie nodded; jaw tight.

"She didn't run."

"She couldn't," Annabel said. "Or maybe she knew... it would be worse if she did."

They walked the rest of the way to Honeystone Cottage in silence.

***

Inside, the kettle clicked on like it always did.

The fire glowed.

Everything looked the same.

But it wasn't.

Annabel sat at the table, fingers curled around a warm mug, staring down at the paper with Agnes's last words.

"She used mine."

Grace leaned forward.

"Do you think she meant Gillian?

She's the only one who said she returned her key *directly* to Agnes."

Evie frowned.

"Could be.

Could be someone else who never gave theirs up.

Could be someone who *took* hers."

"Do you think she knew who it was?" Grace asked.

"She didn't name them," Annabel said. "But she knew."

"She left it in her pew," Evie said. "Not the vicar's office.

Not tucked in a hymnal.

She left it where someone like *us* might sit."

Annabel looked at her.

"Someone who would care enough to look."

***

Persephone leapt onto the windowsill and stared out at the dusk. Her tail twitched once.

"What do we do now?" Grace asked.

136

Evie stood.

"We go back.

To that day.

Every movement. Every person. Every coat, every door, every glance.

We find who had the key.

And we find out what they did with it."

Annabel unfolded the note again.

Three words.

One woman.

A silent cry *written just in time.*

"We don't let her die in whispers."

***

Honeystone Cottage smelled faintly of cinnamon and fury.

They'd cleared the side table near the fire, using an old corkboard Grace had found in a charity shop bin and a stash of Annabel's dried lavender pins that now stabbed neatly into folded bits of notepaper.

Each pin held a name.

Each name held a weight.

***

Gillian Berridge, choir master. Said she returned her key to Agnes. No one remembers Agnes confirming that.

"She's ambitious," Evie said. "Not evil.

But she liked the spotlight.

And if she thought Agnes was going to keep her in the shadows forever..."

"She also knows people's habits," Annabel added. "If anyone could plan around Agnes's schedule..."

***

Barbara Ellington, mayor's wife. Old-school. Believes in tradition and "good optics."

"She had a key once," Grace said.

"Supposedly gave it back. But the vicar said she can't be pressed on sacred matters."

"That's politician for *'I still have it and you can't prove it,'*" Evie muttered.

"She'd want control," Annabel said softly.

"And Agnes was the only one she couldn't manipulate."

***

Nathan, groundskeeper. Quiet. Gentle. "Maybe" still has the key. Unclear.

"I don't see it," Grace said.

"That's why it scares me," Evie replied.

"He knows every inch of that building. If he didn't do it... someone might've *used* him."

***

Unknown woman — 'she'. The person in the note. Someone close. Someone trusted.

"Could it be someone no one knew well?" Grace asked.

"Someone new to the village? Or who returned recently?"

"Or someone who never really left," Annabel said.

They stared at the last pinned note.

Possible medical knowledge.

"She was sedated," Evie said. "We're all but certain now."

"Quickly. No fuss. No screaming. No stumble."

"So... either someone with access to medication," Grace said, "or someone with experience giving injections."

Annabel added a card under it:

Possible Roles

- Former nurse
- Home carer

- Diabetic household member

- Veterinarian

- Hospice or palliative worker

***

The room grew quiet again.

The board didn't speak.

But the silence around it *changed shape.*

Agnes was no longer a victim of misfortune.

She had been *chosen.*

Chapter 13

The back room of Honeystone Cottage was never meant to feel like a museum.

But today, with Grace perched at the edge of the armchair and Evie flipping through Agnes's old community files, it felt like *they were curating grief.*

Annabel opened the final drawer.

Inside: a small plastic folder labelled in Agnes's sharp handwriting:

"SNOWDROP CIRCLE — Previous Years"

She lifted it out carefully.

It wasn't full of anything scandalous.

At first.

Just lists. Activities. Sketches.

Craft instructions for paper snowdrops.

Photos of flower crowns and giggling kids holding lanterns.

Then she flipped to the back.

A single page.

Different paper.

Typed.

Agnes's private notes.

***

"Spring '15.

One child withdrawn. Sudden change in demeanour.

Was once vibrant, now hesitant, quiet. No clear reason given for departure.

Parent said 'not interested anymore.' Didn't sound right."

***

Annabel frowned.

"This wasn't meant for the archive."

Evie leaned over.

"She kept it separate.

Like she didn't want it lost... but didn't want it found either."

Grace stood.

"Spring 2015..."

Her voice dropped.

"That's ten years ago."

They all paused.

Annabel ran her finger under the lines again.

"Do we know who was in the Circle that year?"

Grace bit her lip.

"Rosie's too young...

But if someone was nine or ten then...

They'd be in their late teens or twenties now."

Evie's eyes narrowed.

"Which means they could be anywhere.

Still in the village.

Or came back recently."

"And if Agnes recognised them..." Grace whispered.

"She might've asked too many questions," Annabel finished.

"And someone panicked."

***

The file sat open on the table.

A single snowdrop drawing fluttered loose from the papers, sliding to the floor.

Persephone pawed at it once.

Then sat back.

Watching.

Waiting.

Chapter 14

Gillian Berridge's house smelled like lemon polish and high expectations.

Everything had a place.

Even disappointment, which she stored neatly under a tone of polite condescension.

Evie tapped her foot lightly against the edge of the rug as Gillian rummaged through a wicker filing box.

"I don't know why the vicar didn't keep copies himself," Gillian muttered.

"Honestly, no sense of archiving among clergy. I practically ran the spiritual side of the community, too—just without the sermons."

Annabel smiled thinly.

"We're just trying to piece together some of the older procession and choir lists. Agnes mentioned wanting to bring back some older carols."

"Did she?" Gillian's voice lifted slightly, a flicker of smugness warming her words.

"Well. She could've said so to *me*. We always worked so well together."

Evie said nothing.

She didn't blink.

***

Gillian found a folder labelled "Mistletoe Procession: 2015" and handed it over.

"There. That year was a nightmare. Everything got rescheduled because of a power outage, and the Snowdrop Circle had to rehearse in the parish hall with no heating. Half the kids went home with runny noses and attitudes."

Annabel flipped it open.

Photos.

Choir lists.

Handwritten rotas.

And one laminated newsletter from that winter, folded at the edges.

She paused.

There, in a photo taken in front of the chapel — children in flower crowns, holding candles, eyes bright with winter wonder — was a girl near the back.

No name for this girl.

Just a face.

Dark coat.

Arms folded.

Expression tight.

Eyes not looking at the camera, but past it.

Evie leaned over.

"She doesn't look like she wants to be there."

Gillian made a vague noise.

"Oh. That one."

She waved a hand.

"Family left town not long after. Can't remember the name. Agnes was very concerned, of course. She got... attached."

Grace stepped closer.

"Do you remember anything about her?"

"Not really. One of those kids who always hovered at the edge of the group.

Didn't speak much.

Wore that same coat all the time.

I think it was second-hand."

Evie stared harder at the photo.

"Do you still have your key to the chapel?" she asked, too casually.

Gillian stiffened.

"I told you. I returned it to Agnes."

"Right," Evie said.

"Of course."

***

They left not long after.

The photo, copied and folded into Annabel's notebook, came with them.

So did the memory of that girl's eyes.

Still. Unsmiling. Watching.

Chapter 15

The warmth of Mira's bakery hit Grace like a hug she didn't know she needed.

It smelled like cinnamon and yeast and something faintly floral — the kind of scent you couldn't name but always wanted in your kitchen.

Rosie was sitting at the little corner table, colouring a paper angel, tongue peeking out in concentration.

Grace offered a smile and waved at Mira behind the counter.

"Just popping in for a loaf. If I stay, I'll end up with half the shop."

"As you should," Mira replied, eyes twinkling.

While she wrapped up a seeded sourdough, Mira chatted — about the weather, about candle wax shortages, about the choir sounding like strangled geese last rehearsal.

Then she sighed softly.

"I miss Agnes already."

Grace nodded.

"She was special."

Mira lowered her voice slightly, glancing toward Rosie.

"She cared so much. Especially about the children."

She paused. Then added, more to the bread than to Grace—

"She never let go of that one girl.

The one who left the Circle all of a sudden.

Said something wasn't right.

Used to keep checking in with me years later, asking if I'd heard from the family."

Grace blinked.

"What family?"

Mira shook her head.

"They moved, I think. Just... gone.

But Agnes never believed it was simple.

She used to say, *'Some snowdrops bloom once and disappear. But not because they wanted to.'*"

Grace's fingers tightened around the paper bag.

"Did she ever mention her name?"

"No. Just her eyes. She said they never looked where she was — only through her."

Grace swallowed.

"Thank you, Mira. I'll... I'll see you soon."

She left, heart pounding behind her ribs like a second clock.

***

Later that evening, at Honeystone Cottage, she told Annabel and Evie everything.

Annabel pulled out the photo.

Evie tapped the face of the girl with a pencil.

"We find the name.

We find the girl."

She looked at Grace.

"We know it was in 2015."

Grace nodded.

Evie stood.

"She's not a child anymore.

If she's here... she's hiding something."

Chapter 16

They were still sorting through Agnes's boxes when Persephone decided she'd had enough of being ignored.

She leapt up onto the table, sniffed a pile of pine-scented parchment, and then padded over to a corner of the cardboard lid.

Then she stopped.

Stared.

And extended one paw, delicately batting the folded corner of a snowdrop-shaped craft envelope until it flipped over.

Inside was a single, small name tag — laminated, preserved.

Soft green paper.

Agnes's handwriting.

Curling letters with careful loops.

"Lissie."

Annabel froze.

"Good girl," she whispered.

Evie leaned over; brows drawn.

"That's not on any of the official lists. I checked."

Grace knelt beside the table, touching the corner gently.

"It seems to be a nickname. Not formal. Maybe something only Agnes used."

"Or something *she* asked Agnes to use," Annabel said softly.

Persephone stared at the tag, tail twitching once like a warning.

Evie stood, tension sharpening her words.

"Then we find out who Lissie was.

Before she disappears again."

Chapter 17

The village library smelled like old paper and fresh coffee.

Theo was behind the returns desk, earbuds in, methodically scanning barcodes and stacking books like truths too neat to speak aloud.

Grace hovered near the reference shelves.

Annabel gave her a tiny nod.

"Theo?" she asked gently.

He looked up, startled, pulling out one earbud.

"Oh—Miss Grace. Hi."

"Hi. Do you have a minute?"

He glanced at the quiet clock near the large-print section.

"Yeah. Break in five, actually."

They found a corner by the tall windows.

Evie stayed leaning against a shelf nearby — not quite looming, not quite not.

Annabel opened her notebook. Slipped the snowdrop photo halfway into view.

"Do you remember the Snowdrop Circle? Back in 2015?"

Theo nodded slowly.

"Yeah. I was seven. I remember Agnes... and the crafts. The candle walk.

We made the worst snowdrop garlands that year. Mine looked like onions."

Grace smiled faintly.

"Do you remember a girl named Lissie?"

That was the moment his eyes changed.

Not fear.

Not confusion.

Something closer to regret.

"Yeah," he said quietly.

"Lissie."

***

He didn't speak for a few seconds.

Just looked out the window like the past might be sitting outside on the bench in a puff coat and wool hat.

"She was quiet.

Like… she didn't want to be there, but she wanted to try.

Her hands always shook when we did crafts. I remember that."

"Do you remember her last name?" Annabel asked gently.

Theo shook his head.

"Never knew it. We didn't use surnames in the Circle.

Just our first names and snowdrop nicknames.

Agnes gave me the name 'Frostleaf.'"

He blushed slightly.

"I hated it. But Lissie... she liked hers."

"Which was?" Grace asked.

"Whisperbell."

He smiled, small and sad.

"Said it sounded like a secret no one could break."

Evie's voice came from behind the shelf.

"Did something happen to her, Theo?"

He didn't look away from the window.

"One day she stopped showing up.

Agnes told us her family had to move suddenly."

A pause.

"But Agnes was... weird after that.

Like she kept waiting for her to come back.

Kept checking the Circle sign-ups every year.

Even asked me once — three years later — if I'd 'heard from Whisperbell.'"

He looked down.

"I didn't. I never did."

***

They thanked him. Quietly.

On the way out, Grace held the notebook tighter against her chest.

"Whisperbell," she whispered.

"A snowdrop secret."

Evie glanced up at the grey sky.

"She had a nickname.

She had a fear.

And now... she has a trail."

Chapter 18

They found Nora in her garden shed, where she was repotting something aggressively into an oversized tin bucket.

Persephone sat on the windowsill behind her, tail curled neatly, eyes unblinking.

"What are you lot doing, digging around in winter like badgers?"

"Historical research," Annabel said smoothly.

"On what?"

"Housing turnover in the village. Around 10 years ago, so around 2015," Grace added.

"Oh, real thrilling stuff," Nora snorted.

"I hope there's a prize involved."

***

She set her trowel down and brushed off her gloves, leading them inside to the kitchen — which smelled like lemon biscuits and faint suspicion.

From under a tea towel in the sideboard, she produced *The Book*.

"It's not official, obviously," she said.

"But when people move out suddenly, it helps to know who owed what to the jumble sale."

She flipped to the 2015 section.

"Let's see... Meredith sold her place in spring, but that was expected — her third husband hated daffodils.

And... ah. *Here.* This one's funny."

Her finger landed on a line:

No. 7, Mulberry Lane – Tenant: Harper. Moved out March 2015. Sudden. No notice. No forwarding.

"That was odd," Nora said, tapping the margin.

"Single mum. Young. Kept to herself. Had a little girl. Quiet one.

Can't for the life of me remember their first names — it was always *'the Harper girl.'*"

Evie stiffened.

"Did anyone know why they left?"

Nora leaned in like a cat about to push over a vase.

"Rumour was the landlord got fed up. Something about missed payments, police knocking about once, I don't know."

"But I remember Agnes... she was upset. Not the kind of upset you can fix with tea."

Annabel's heart was thudding now.

"Did the little girl go to the Snowdrop Circle?"

"Every week," Nora said. "Until she didn't.

And you know what's funny?"

No one breathed.

"Agnes gave me a snowdrop crown to deliver to her the day after they left.

She didn't think they'd be coming to the final procession.

Said *'She deserves to bloom, even if no one's there to see it.'*"

Chapter 19

The house at No. 7 Mulberry Lane looked like it had been politely scrubbed of history.

New curtains. Fresh paint. No visible ghosts.

But Annabel knew — the ghosts always hid under the floorboards, or in the glances between neighbours.

They knocked on the door of No. 9 next door — a tidy cottage with a ceramic duck in the flowerbed.

A woman in a cobalt blue cardigan answered, clutching a mug with *"Let it Scone"* printed on it.

"Can I help you?"

"Hello!" Annabel said brightly. "We're doing a bit of village history research. Looking at migration trends — families who moved out over the past ten years."

"Oh, are you with the local council?"

"No, just... curious," Grace smiled. "Especially about this lane. Seems like a quiet place."

The woman relaxed.

"Well, it is now," she said. "Used to be livelier.

No. 7 had a family in it, back in 2015 or so.

Young mother. Quiet girl. Didn't get many visitors."

"Do you remember their names?" Annabel asked gently.

"The mum was Harper, I think. First name... Claire? Clara? Something like that. The little girl was shy. Wouldn't talk to anyone but that choir lady—Agnes, was it?"

They all nodded.

The woman took a sip of her tea.

"Then one day — poof. Gone.

Took their things and left in the night.

Landlord was furious. Said the rent was late, but... I don't know."

"Why do you say that?" Evie asked.

The woman lowered her voice.

"There were... sounds. Arguments. Once or twice, I thought I heard crying late.

And one night, a car pulled up, and someone was shouting. Not her, though.

She just stood there on the step."

A pause.

"The little girl was clutching a paper flower crown.

Wouldn't let it go."

Chapter 20

The chapel smelled of stone, candle wax, and a hush so old it had its own weight.

Reverend Harrow met them at the vestry door, sleeves rolled, spectacles perched halfway down his nose.

"Miss Grace. Miss Annabel. I take it this isn't just for the history fair?"

Annabel gave a small smile.

"We're... looking into a past family. From 2015.

Harper. Claire, and a little girl."

The vicar didn't blink. Just stepped back and gestured toward the records cabinet.

"Let's see what the walls remember."

***

The register was thick. Bound in soft leather.

The pages whispered when turned — thin and reverent.

He flipped to the 2015 section.

Ran his finger down a column. Then stopped.

"Claire Harper. Attended the parish briefly that winter. No christening, but she did register her daughter for the Mistletoe Blessing."

He turned the page.

"Here."

There it was.

Child's name: *Elisabetta May Harper*

Preferred name: *Lissie*

Note: *"Asked to be listed under nickname. Insisted."*

Grace read the words again and again, as though they'd vanish if she blinked.

"Elisabetta," she whispered.

"She didn't just vanish. She existed. She *asked* to be remembered a certain way."

"She stood right there," the vicar said softly. "Tiny thing. Clutched her mother's hand like she was afraid the air might take her."

Annabel traced the edge of the entry with her finger.

It was just ink on parchment. But it felt like *a lifeline, reaching backward.*

"Did anything happen?" she asked.

Reverend Harrow was quiet for a long time.

Then:

"Claire Harper came to me once.

Asked if the chapel offered any kind of... sanctuary."

"Sanctuary?" Grace echoed.

"Said she was afraid. Didn't say of what. Or who.

Just that she needed somewhere safe.

I told her she'd always be welcome here."

He closed the book gently.

"But two days later… they were gone."

***

Outside, the wind stirred through the graveyard.

Snowdrops were not blooming yet — but the ground knew they were coming.

Persephone sat just beyond the chapel door, staring at the stone steps.

She didn't move as they came out.

Just flicked her tail once — a gesture that felt like punctuation.

Grace spoke first; voice low.

"Do you think Benedict knows?"

Annabel frowned.

"It could be coincidence. Harper isn't rare."

"But it's Little Firling. We're not drowning in Harpers."

She stopped. Looked down at the chapel path.

"Agnes tried to help her. She asked for sanctuary."

Annabel's throat tightened.

"She gave it. In every way she could."

They walked back toward the village in silence, each carrying something new:

A name. A grief. A purpose.

And maybe — just maybe — a girl who never stopped whispering.

Chapter 21

Benedict Harper lived in a narrow red-brick cottage with ivy climbing the front like it was searching for something.

The curtains were always drawn just enough to keep the world out — but never so much that he couldn't see the world trying to peer in.

He opened the door with a slight smile when Annabel and Grace appeared.

"Didn't expect visitors," he said. "But you've got that look that says it's not about jam sales or herb swaps."

"We were hoping you might have a moment," Grace said.

"Course. Come in."

***

His home was quiet. Clean. Books lined the fireplace wall. A kettle rumbled to life in the background.

Persephone slipped in behind them and curled immediately on the rug — like she'd always belonged there.

"What's this about?" Benedict asked, settling into the armchair with a slow exhale.

"Something to do with Agnes, I imagine."

Annabel sat opposite him.

"Do you remember a woman named Claire Harper?"

His brow furrowed.

"That's... a name I haven't heard in years."

Grace leaned forward.

"She lived on Mulberry Lane. Had a daughter. Elisabetta — she went by Lissie.

They left suddenly in 2015."

Benedict looked down at his hands, quiet for a beat.

"I didn't know her well. I do not think that we were related."

"Did you ever meet her?" Annabel asked.

"Once. Briefly. At a chapel gathering, I think.

She looked tired. Edges worn thin.

The sort of person who'd already packed her bags in her head even when she walked into a room."

He swallowed hard.

"I remember Agnes talking to her. With that voice she had... the one that made you feel safe even when you weren't.

And then... they were gone."

Grace shifted in her seat.

"Did Agnes ever tell you why she cared so much about them?"

"Not directly. But I know she kept checking. Hoping.

I think... she thought the girl might come back one day.

That maybe she'd walk through the chapel doors with a crown in her hand and forgiveness in her eyes."

He looked up.

"Why now? Why ask me?"

Annabel hesitated.

"Because Agnes left a note. A message.

And it started with someone using her key.

But now it feels like it ends with Lissie."

Chapter 22

The current tenants of No. 7 had only just moved in the previous month — a retired couple restoring the garden. They'd found the house "charming," though "oddly echoey."

When Grace asked politely if they might look inside for "archival interest in the house's village history," the wife had nodded.

"Only fair," she'd said. "This house still hums like it's holding its breath."

***

Inside, the cottage was warm, half-painted, still in that half-settled stage where the past hadn't quite let go.

Annabel drifted toward the old built-in bookcase in the hallway.

Grace checked the airing cupboard.

Evie wandered toward the small bedroom in the back — once a child's, maybe.

Persephone came too.

Silent.

Certain.

*   *   *

It was Grace who found it.

Behind the tall wardrobe, where the floorboard dipped, a narrow tin box had wedged between wall and floor. Dusty. Unmarked. Cold.

She pulled it out gently and called the others.

Inside:

A crumpled drawing — a snowdrop crown, uneven petals shaded in blue

A paper programme from the 2015 Mistletoe Procession rehearsal

And at the very bottom — a photograph.

The girl stood slightly off-centre. Not smiling.

Brown coat. Messy fringe. One sock higher than the other.

Her hands were at her sides — one holding a small cat figurine, like she didn't realise.

"That's her," Annabel breathed.

"Lissie."

Evie stared. Her voice was a whisper.

"She looks like she's trying to disappear."

Grace pulled the drawing up again. The snowdrops had names under them. One said:

"Lissie W."

The last letter blurred, but not enough.

"That's not May," Annabel said.

"No," Grace replied. "That's not 'May' at all."

Evie picked up the photograph.

"But it's her."

***

They stood in silence, surrounded by new paint and old sorrow.

Persephone brushed her paw once over the edge of the paper crown and then curled beside the tin.

Watching.

Waiting.

Chapter 23

The bakery smelled of cardamom and toasted almonds, as if every loaf was whispering warmth into the grey of winter.

Grace and Annabel entered together; the photograph of Lissie tucked into the inner flap of Annabel's notebook like a secret between old pages.

Mira was at the counter, apron dusted in flour, hair pinned up with a red pencil.

She looked up and smiled.

"Back again. Thought you'd be halfway through that sourdough by now."

"We're rationing it carefully," Annabel replied, her smile small but real.

"Mira... do you have a moment?"

The sparkle in Mira's eyes softened.

"I always have time for the curious kind."

***

They sat at the corner table while Mira poured tea, her movements smooth and practiced, as if warmth itself was something you could shape like dough.

Annabel placed the photo gently on the table between them.

"We're trying to find her. Her name was Elisabetta Harper.

She went by Lissie.

She left the village in 2015.

Or… we thought she did."

Mira's hand, halfway to her mug, stopped.

She stared at the photo.

And then said — very softly:

"That's Willow."

Grace blinked.

"Willow?"

"She goes by Willow now. Came back a few months ago.

Told me she was house-sitting.

Brought her own tea bags. Doesn't like rye flour.

But the first time I saw, she was holding a snowdrop biscuit…"

Mira swallowed.

"She froze.

Like she wasn't in the bakery anymore."

***

A long silence. Only the clink of spoons in distant mugs.

"Where is she staying?" Annabel asked gently.

"Number Three. Wisteria Cottage. Just past the old bramble fence.

Her window lights are on late. Always late.

Like someone still waiting for something they don't believe is coming."

Mira touched the edge of the photo.

"That's her.

But she's changed."

"So have we," Grace said.

Chapter 24

Back at Honeystone Cottage, the photo lay between the teacups like an open wound.

Persephone was curled by the fire, one ear twitching as if keeping time with unspoken thoughts.

Evie sat on the arm of the chair, arms crossed, eyes sharp.

"So, she came back. Changed her name. Settled in like no one would notice."

"She didn't go to Agnes's funeral," Grace murmured.

Annabel nodded slowly.

"And Mira said she froze when she saw a snowdrop biscuit."

"She didn't just change her name," Evie said.

"She tried to bury it."

Grace looked at the photo again.

The child and the woman were different — but not *disconnected.*

"Do you think... Agnes found her?"

"If she did," Annabel said, "what did she say?"

Evie stared into the fire.

"She asked for sanctuary in 2015.

Maybe she came back to see if it was still here."

Grace looked up.

"Or maybe she came back because *she was afraid* Agnes would tell someone."

A pause.

"If she did something.

If something *happened.*"

***

Evie spoke next. Carefully.

"You don't hide your name unless you're hiding something."

"But do you kill for it?" Grace asked.

Silence.

Only the crackle of the fire. And the soft, rhythmic purring of Persephone, like a second heartbeat.

"It depends," Annabel said finally.

"On what Agnes remembered.

And what Willow couldn't bear to hear again."

Chapter 25

It was supposed to be a quiet afternoon.

Willow had only wanted oatcakes and solitude.

But as she stepped out of the bakery, brown paper bag in hand, a voice called out behind her.

"Lissie?"

She froze.

It wasn't shouted.

It wasn't even sharp.

Just... soft. Surprised.

But too familiar.

She turned slowly.

Mara.

Older now. Taller. Confident in a way that made Willow's spine stiffen.

"Sorry?" Willow said, voice calm, even.

"Sorry," Mara laughed, shaking her head. "It's just—those eyes.

You look just like someone I knew when we were kids."

Willow smiled — tight, polite, all edges.

"Common face, I suppose."

"No... it's not." Mara tilted her head.

"You used to draw snowdrops with five petals.

Always five. You said the sixth one was unlucky."

Willow gripped the paper bag harder.

"I think you've mistaken me."

Mara's smile faded just slightly.

"Where are you staying? Do you know anyone in the village?"

"I'm house-sitting. That's all."

"Married?"

Willow blinked.

"Why?"

"Just wondering if anyone... knows you're back."

A silence stretched between them.

And then Willow turned.

Walked away.

Fast.

Too fast.

Mara watched her go.

Then reached into her coat pocket, pulled out her phone...

And opened her messages.

To: Grace

"*She's here. And she remembers more than she wants to admit.*"

Chapter 26

Some people think you change your name and that's the hardest part.

It's not.

The hardest part is *hearing your old one again.*

From someone whose voice once shared the same paper scissors, the same cold floor, the same choir song.

The hardest part is *remembering what your name used to mean.*

Before it was a secret.

***

Willow sat at the edge of the bed in Wisteria Cottage.

She hadn't turned the light on.

The paper bag from the bakery sat unopened beside her.

Her coat was still on.

Her hands were ice.

She could still hear Mara's voice.

"You used to draw snowdrops with five petals."

She used to.

She also used to believe her mother's name was Claire.

***

But Claire Harper wasn't her mother.

Willow knew that now.

She wasn't sure when she'd *first* known it, but it was a knowledge that had grown like a splinter under the skin — small, painful, and impossible to ignore once it reached bone.

Claire wasn't cruel.

Not exactly.

But she'd *kept secrets like locks.*

And *loved with rules.*

And *left in the night without ever saying why.*

****

Agnes had been different.

Agnes saw her. Even when she didn't want to be seen.

Agnes made snowdrops out of paper and words.

She'd said once, *"Some people bloom once and think that's all they get. But winter always ends, sweetheart."*

Willow had believed her. For a while.

Until the letters started.

Until the questions came back.

Until she'd walked into the chapel again — *just to see if it remembered her.*

And *Agnes was waiting.*

***

She hadn't threatened her.

She'd said *she knew.*

And *that she forgave.*

And *that Willow didn't have to keep running.*

But someone else was listening.

Someone *who didn't want forgiveness.*

***

Willow's hands shook now as she unwrapped the paper bag.

The oatcakes crumbled slightly in her lap.

Outside, the wind moved the cottage shutters.

Inside, she finally whispered her own name.

"Lissie."

It didn't sound like guilt.

It sounded like *mourning.*

***

Willow sat on the bench under the beech tree, sketchpad on her lap.

She wasn't drawing flowers this time.

She was drawing *a hallway. Narrow. Cold. With wallpaper that peeled in the corners.*

Her fingers worked in silence, but her breath was tight.

A shadow passed behind her.

Not close.

Not lingering.

Just... there.

Marian Pettifer.

Carrying a woven basket, a bunch of rosemary tucked beneath her arm.

She didn't speak.

She only glanced once — at the sketchpad — and kept walking.

But her eyes stayed fixed too long.

And her face never changed.

Willow didn't notice.

But Persephone, sitting a few feet away, flicked her tail once.

Like punctuation.

Chapter 27

Willow was sketching again.

This time, it was a face.

Not clear.

Not precise.

But familiar in the way *a scent can shatter a memory.*

Soft jaw. Thin mouth.

Hair tied back with navy ribbon.

And a hand — holding out a biscuit.

Smiling.

***

Outside, the air felt wrong.

Still.

Too still.

Like the pause before a page turns.

Persephone sat on the windowsill.

Watching.

Tail curled tight.

Then, she dropped down and padded to the door.

A knock.

Soft. Rhythmic. Familiar.

Willow opened the door.

***

Marian Pettifer stood there in her dove-grey coat.

No basket today.

Only gloves, clean.

And a scarf too perfectly folded.

"Hello, dear. I was just... passing by.

I saw you sketching the other day."

Willow didn't answer.

But her hand curled around the pencil behind her back.

"I remember when you used to draw. Even then, you had such... detail.

So much memory in your fingertips."

"You watched me," Willow whispered.

"I protected you." Marian's voice was a lullaby lined with frost.

"From people who didn't deserve you."

"You took me," Willow said.

"You helped her."

"You were suffering. And I gave you peace."

"And then... Agnes wanted to bring it all back."

She stepped forward.

"I couldn't let her ruin everything. Not after all these years. Not after everything I gave."

Willow stepped back.

"You killed her."

Marian didn't blink.

"I let her sleep.

I let the cold do the rest.

I left her with the snowdrops."

Her hand slipped into her coat pocket.

Something shimmered — small, silver.

A syringe.

***

But before she could move—

"Stop right there."

Grace's voice cut through the doorway like bells before dawn.

Behind her, Annabel. And Evie.

And Persephone, perched at the threshold.

Growling.

***

Marian's eyes flicked from Willow to the women.

Then down to the floor.

She smiled.

It was almost fond.

"You wouldn't understand.

She was blooming again.

And I couldn't let her bloom *wrong*."

***

The police came quietly.

Barbara never came out of the house that day.

But the next morning, the mayor resigned.

And a new bouquet was left on the chapel steps.

Paper snowdrops.

Folded by Willow.

Each one with six petals.

Epilogue

The snow came late that year.

It dusted the rooftops of Little Firling like powdered sugar, settling between cottage chimneys and quiet grave markers.

On the chapel steps, someone had placed *a single, real snowdrop* in a jar. No name. No card. Just truth.

Inside Honeystone Cottage, the fire crackled softly.

***

"The report came in this morning," Grace said, setting the envelope on the table.

"Full name: Marian Pettifer. Fifty-nine. Former child welfare officer. Sister of Barbara Ellington."

Annabel poured tea.

Evie crossed her arms, jaw tight.

"Retired early. No charges, but the department filed her under 'boundary concerns.'

They said she'd grown too close to a few cases."

Grace read aloud:

"In 2009, she made contact with a woman named Claire, who had been denied adoption rights after multiple failed assessments.

Claire 'wanted a child more than anything.'

Marian 'wanted to save a child from a broken home.'"

"So, they took her," Annabel said quietly.

"They brought her here.

Claire changed her name. Marian falsified records.

They told Willow she'd always lived in Little Firling. That her recollections were just dreams."

***

Evie exhaled.

"And Marian believed she'd done a good thing."

"Until Willow came back.

And Agnes started trying to reconnect with her."

They sat in silence.

Even Persephone, curled by the window, was still.

***

Outside, the chapel bells rang.

They walked there together.

Willow stood by the Virgin statue, a fresh snowdrop crown in her hands.

Her sketchpad tucked beneath one arm.

She turned when they approached.

Smiled.

"She called me Lissie," she said softly.

"But I think my name is Willow.

That's the name I gave myself.

That's the one I want to keep."

Grace reached for her hand.

"Then that's who you are."

***

Barbara Ellington had left the village.

No one said much.

Her house sat empty, but flowers appeared on its steps every few days.

Forgiveness, maybe. Or guilt.

The letter was folded neatly now.

No creases. No tears.

She'd read it three times that morning—

And it still didn't feel real.

Grace sat on the bench behind the chapel, scarf tucked under her chin, the paper clutched in woollen gloves. The snow had begun to melt in little patches, revealing frostbitten grass beneath.

She could hear voices from the green. A child laughing. A door shutting gently.

But here, in the hush, she let herself breathe.

"You were wanted," Agnes had written.

Not just a kindness.

Not just a phrase.

A *correction* of something that had lived inside her too long.

She'd been told, over the years, that her father hadn't been "in the picture."

That he had gone.

That he hadn't known what to do with a baby.

"He was a good man, just not ready," they said.

"Some people just... leave."

So, she learned not to ask.

But she also learned — quietly, cruelly — to believe that *she wasn't enough to make someone stay.*

And that maybe, just maybe, *she hadn't been worth the fight.*

But this letter...

Agnes hadn't said it with pity.

She'd said it with *knowing.*

"You were dreamed about."

Grace looked down again.

Agnes had known something.

Not everything, maybe—

But *enough to carry it like a prayer.*

And that line—

"Some things bloom once, and never stop echoing."

She wiped her face on her sleeve.

She wasn't a secret anymore.

She wasn't a regret.

She was a snowdrop.

And she was finally blooming again.

****

The sketchpad sat open on the table.

She hadn't meant to draw it.

It just happened.

A room she hadn't seen in years. A window with a curtain too short. A door with three locks, even though it was inside the house.

She stared at the lines for a long time.

Not afraid. Not anymore.

Across from her, Persephone watched from the windowsill.

Tail flicking. Eyes half-lidded.

As if to say, *"Well, it's about time."*

Willow smiled faintly.

"I remember now."

The voice that told her to be quiet.

The one that told her she was lucky.

The one that said the past wasn't important.

It wasn't Claire's voice.

It was Marian's.

"You were meant to be safe," Marian had whispered.

"You were meant to stay hidden."

But safety had felt like shrinking.

And hiding had never felt like home.

Willow looked down at the page.

She picked up her pencil.

And beside the door with the locks, she drew a new window.

Bigger. Brighter. Open.

***

"My name is Willow," she whispered to herself.

"And I am mine."

***

That spring, the snowdrop crowns were made with six petals.

Not because they were unlucky.

But because they told the whole truth.

And that year, the procession walked slower.

Not in mourning.

But in reverence.

Because *sometimes the quietest stories are the ones that bloom loudest in the end.*

***

Honeystone Cottage smelled like cinnamon, orange peel, and something faintly singed.

"I told you that oven runs hot," Annabel muttered, waving a tea towel at the smoke alarm.

"It does not like mince pies."

"The pies are perfect," Evie said, already biting into one, mouth full. "Crunchy on the outside, rebellion on the inside. Just like us."

Annabel rolled her eyes but smiled, finally letting herself sit down.

Persephone made a grand leap from the armchair to the centre of the table, knocked over a pinecone, sniffed the wreath, and dramatically flopped onto the only clean placemat.

"Absolutely not," Annabel said. "You are *not* the centrepiece."

Persephone blinked. Slowly. Like a queen unbothered by the complaints of mere peasants.

"She is the unsolved mystery in this house," Evie said, stroking the cat's head. "And I'm not sure we'll ever catch her."

Outside, the snow fell softly and slowly, like someone had remembered to be gentle.

Inside, the fire crackled.

Willow had stopped by earlier, just long enough to leave them a sketch: a single snowdrop blooming on a windowsill.

It now sat framed on the mantel.

***

"We've seen a lot this year," Annabel said softly.

"More than I expected when I planted tomatoes last spring."

"And yet, here we are," Evie replied, raising her teacup.

"Alive. Untangled. And in possession of twelve extra mince pies."

"Ten," Annabel corrected.

"Five," Evie admitted.

They both laughed.

Persephone purred.

And somewhere outside, in the village quiet, a bell rang — not to warn or mourn this time, but simply to say:

We made it.